For Mom and Dad,
with gratitude and love, through every season.—D. W.

For Sara, Tom, Luca, Ester, Mattia,
Claudia, Francesco, and those still to come.—F. S.

BEACH LANE BOOKS
An imprint of Simon & Schuster Children's Publishing Division
1230 Avenue of the Americas, New York, New York 10020
Text copyright © 2020 by Dianne White
Illustrations copyright © 2020 by Felicita Sala
BEACH LANE BOOKS is a trademark of Simon & Schuster, Inc.
For information about special discounts for bulk purchases, please contact Simon & Schuster Special Sales
at 1-866-506-1949 or business@simonandschuster.com.
The Simon & Schuster Speakers Bureau can bring authors to your live event.
For more information or to book an event, contact the Simon & Schuster Speakers Bureau
at 1-866-248-3049 or visit our website at www.simonspeakers.com.
Book design by Lauren Rille
The text for this book was set in The Hand.
The illustrations for this book were rendered in watercolor, gouache, and colored pencils.
Manufactured in China
0721 SCP
10 9 8 7 6 5 4
Library of Congress Cataloging-in-Publication Data
Names: White, Dianne, author. | Sala, Felicita, illustrator. • Title: Green on green / Dianne White ; illustrated by Felicita Sala. • Description: First edition. |
New York : Beach Lane Books, [2020] | Summary: Illustrations and simple, rhyming text highlight the animals, fruits, feelings, and colors that characterize
each season of the year. • Identifiers: LCCN 2019009181 | ISBN 9781481462785 (hardcover) | ISBN 9781481462792 (eBook) • Subjects: | CYAC: Stories
in rhyme. | Color—Fiction. | Seasons—Fiction. | Nature—Fiction. • Classification: LCC PZ8.3.W58735 Gr 2020 | DDC [E]—dc23 LC record available at
https://lccn.loc.gov/2019009181

Dianne White   Felicita Sala

GREEN ON GREEN

BEACH LANE BOOKS • New York London Toronto Sydney New Delhi

Yellow the flower.
Yellow the seed.
Yellow and black the buzzing bee.

Lemonade petals.
Sunflakes between.
Lemonade, sunflakes, and yellow on green.

Spring the meadow.
Spring the pond.
Spring the season of new birds' song.

Gentle the breezes.
Rain between.
Breezes and rain and yellow on green.

Blue the coral.
Blue the shell.
Blue and white the foaming swell.

Turquoise the water.
Teal between.
Turquoise, teal, and blue on green.

Summer the picnic.
Summer the peach.
Summer the season of wave and beach.

Endless the sun.
Shade between.
Sun and shade and blue on green.

Brown the squirrel.
Brown the mouse.
Brown the trees around our house.

Cinnamon spice.
Almond between.
Cinnamon, almond, and brown on green.

Fall the pumpkin.
Fall the corn.
Fall the season of toasty and warm.

Friends round the table.
Candles between.
Table and candles and brown on green.

White the breath.
White the snow.
White and black the cawing crow.

Gray the sky.
Taupe between.
Gray and taupe and white on green.

Winter the sparkle.
Winter the chill.
Winter the season of hope and goodwill.

Peaceful the evening.
Pine between.
Evening and pine and green . . .

on green.